This Book Belongs To

. . . .

Text copyright © 1999 Margaret Ryan
Illustrations copyright © 1999 Andy Ellis

This edition first published 1999
by Hodder Children's Books

A Catalogue record for this book is available from the
British Library

ISBN 0 340 73984 3

Printed and bound in Great Britain by The Devonshire
Press, Torquay, Devon TQ2 7NX

Hodder Children's Books
a division of Hodder Headline plc
338 Euston Road
London NW1 3BH

Little Blue
in a mess

Margaret Ryan

illustrated by Andy Ellis

Hodder
Children's
Books

a division of Hodder Headline plc

For Peter
with love - M.R.

For Max
- A.E.

It was a fine sunny afternoon
and Little Blue was making
mud castles on the sea shore.
"I like mud," said Little Blue.

"Splishy mud, splashy mud,
splodgy mud! Any kind of
mud so long as it's squishy
and squelchy."

He piled more mud on his castle and gave it three doors made of pebbles and two flags made of paper and sticks.

"There," he said. "That looks really good."

"And YOU look really messy,
Little Blue," said his mum,
waddling out of the old
upturned boat where they
lived. "You'd better get
cleaned up before Auntie Pen
comes for tea. You know she
likes clean little penguins."

"Do I HAVE to get clean?" said
Little Blue. "I like messy.

"Yes, you have to get clean,"
said his mum. "Come inside.
Right now."
"Okay," muttered Little Blue,
and trailed indoors after
his mum.

4

First Little Blue's mum
cleaned his face.

"I know there's a little blue
penguin somewhere
underneath all this mud,"
she said.

"Ooh, ow, ouch, stop it! I hate soap up my nose," said Little Blue.

Then Little Blue's mum
cleaned his feet.

"Where have you been with
these feet, Little Blue?" she
said. "They're black!"

"Ooh, ow, ouch, they're
SUPPOSED to be black. Don't
scrub my skin off," said
Little Blue.

Finally Little Blue's mum
cleaned his flippers.
"Don't flap about so much,"
she said.

"Can't help it," giggled Little
Blue. "That tickles."

"There," said his mum. "That looks a lot better. Now, Auntie Pen will be here soon. Remember to stay clean."

Little Blue tried to stay clean,
but it wasn't easy. He sat on
the upturned boat and had a
think about it.

"How can I keep my face clean," he said, "when I don't know how it gets dirty? Perhaps if I tuck it under my flipper that will keep it clean."

So he tucked his face under
his flipper.

"Ooh, it's dark in here,"
he said.

It was so dark he couldn't see
where he was going. He took
two steps forward and fell
over.
"Help!"

Little Blue picked himself up
and dusted off the sand
and pebbles. "Well that's no
good," he said, and had
another think.

"How can I keep my feet
clean," he said, "when I don't
know how they get dirty?
Perhaps if I just stand on one
foot at a time they won't get
dirty so quickly."
So he stood on his left foot.

WIBBLE WOBBLE WIBBLE.

He fell over.

He stood on his right foot.
WIBBLE WOBBLE WIBBLE.

He fell over again.

17

He picked himself up
and dusted off the sand
and pebbles.

"Well that's no good either,"
he said.

"What's no good, Little Blue?"
asked his friend, Rocky, the
rockhopper penguin, hopping
up beside him.

"Trying to stay clean because
Auntie Pen's coming for tea,"
said Little Blue.

"Staying clean's easy!" said
Rocky. "Come for a swim,
Little Blue. You'll be nice and
clean after that."

"Good idea," said Little Blue
and hopped down to
the ocean.

Little Blue and Rocky played
and swam until Little Blue
was as clean as a penguin
could be.

"That was fun, Rocky," said
Little Blue. "But I'd better go
home now, in case Auntie Pen
has arrived."

He said goodbye to Rocky and was just about to swim ashore when two dark triangular shapes appeared in the water.

"Oh no," said Little Blue. "It's the sharks, Fick and Fin. They're between me and the shore and I think they've spotted me!"

They had.
They swam a little closer.
"Do you see what I see, Fick?"
said Fin.

"I see the sea, Fin," said Fick.
"Apart from that," said Fin.
"Let me see," said Fick. "Oh, I
know, I see that tasty little
blue penguin, Fin."

"We could sneak up on him and have him for afternoon tea," said Fin.
"So long as he hasn't been playing in the mud again," said Fick.

"I've never SEEN such a messy penguin."
"Let's chase him and see."
And they swam swiftly towards Little Blue, teeth bared and ready.

"Oh no," cried Little Blue.
"SHARK ATTACK,
SHARK ATTACK!

Now I'll have to dive down
through the seaweed tunnels
to get home. It's too narrow in
there for the sharks to follow."

26

He dived down and swam
through the seaweed tunnels.
Just in time!

It was scary in there. Big eyes
blinked at him from
black holes.

Big claws nipped at him
from black rocks. And there
was LOTS of seaweed.

Slippy seaweed, sloppy
seaweed, slimy seaweed. It
clung to the walls. It hung
from the roof.

It curled itself round and
round Little Blue as he
swam past.

"Oh no," he said, when he finally got to the shore.

"Just look at me! I'm covered in seaweed and I was supposed to stay clean. NOW what am I going to do?"

Little Blue waddled up the
beach and sat down on a rock
at the edge of the parkland.
He was just having another
think when his pal, Joey the
little kangaroo, hopped up.

"Hullo, Little Blue," he said. "Been in the seaweed tunnels?

"Yes," said Little Blue. "I had to go through them to get away from Fick and Fin. But now look at me! I was supposed to stay clean for Auntie Pen. She's coming for tea and she likes clean little penguins."

"Never mind," said Joey.
"Come with me and have a
roll around in the dust. That
always gives us kangaroos a
good clean."

"Good idea," said Little Blue
and hopped as fast as he could
to keep up with Joey.

"Look," said Joey. "This is what you do." And he lay on his back on the ground and rolled from side to side.

"And that gets you clean?" asked Little Blue.
"It works for kangaroos," said Joey. "Try it."

Little Blue tried it.
ROLY POLY ROLY POLY.
It was great fun. They were both just having a good roll around when there was a noise like distant thunder.

"Oh no," said Joey. "It's Big Grey and his mob. Quick, Little Blue, jump into the swamp before those big kangaroos knock us over!"

"Oh no, not into the smelly swamp," said Little Blue. "Jump," yelled Joey. "NOW!"

Little Blue and Joey jumped into the swamp, just in time, as Big Grey and his mob thundered past.

"Did you see that little blue penguin as we went past?" Big Grey asked his mob.
"Little fellow, black head, blue chest, hangs out with Joey?" they said.

"That's him," said Big Grey.
"Didn't see him," said his mob.
"No, neither did I," said Big Grey.

"Whew," said Joey. "That was a lucky escape. Time I hopped back to my mum and into her pouch for tea."

"Tea!" cried Little Blue. "Oh no, Auntie Pen's coming for tea, and I was supposed to stay clean."

"Looks like you blew it, Little Blue," giggled Joey, and hopped away.

"NOW what am I going to do?" said Little Blue. "I tried to stay clean, but all that happened was I got covered in seaweed and dust and smelly swamp mud. Mum will be hopping mad."

Suddenly there was a flash of lightning and a rumble of thunder. REAL thunder. Big black clouds appeared and big fat raindrops plopped down on Little Blue.

"Hooray hooray," shouted
Little Blue, and danced about
in the rain. "Now I can get
clean again!"
He danced about till his face
was clean, his feet were clean
and his flippers were
sparkling.
"Now I can go home," he said.
"Now I'm as clean as a
penguin can be. Mum WILL
be pleased."

She was. So was Auntie Pen.
"Well done, Little Blue," she
said. "You managed to stay
clean today."

"No problem," said Little Blue,
giving Auntie Pen his biggest
smile."I stayed clean especially
for you."

"Well, I think you deserve a little treat," said Auntie Pen. "Look what I brought for you."

And she took from her bag the biggest, creamiest, chocolate mud cake Little Blue had ever seen.

"My favourite," grinned Little
Blue. "Thank you very much,
Auntie Pen."
He leaned forward, took the
big cake in his clean flippers,
tripped over his clean feet
and stuck his clean face right
into it.

He came up messy, but smiling. "It tastes delicious," he said. "And you can't possibly eat chocolate mud cake and stay clean, can you?"